Chapter 1

"Heads up!"

The Bertolizzi family looked up from their picnic just in time to see a football sailing toward them.

"I got it!" Alfie shouted, catching the ball right before it landed in the penne-pasta salad. "Maybe I should play football instead of soccer," he said, grinning.

A teenage boy from across the park waved his hand for the ball. "Sorry!" he called. Alfie gave the football his best pass back. It wobbled through the air and landed short.

"I think you should stick with soccer." Alfie's big sister, Emilia, laughed.

Alfie gave Emilia's shoulder a playful nudge. The

Giada De Laurentiis's

Recipe for Adventure

New Orleans!

illustrated by Francesca Gambatesa

Grosset & Dunlap
An Imprint of Penguin Group (USA) LLC

I'd like to dedicate this book to the people of New Orleans,
who always inspire me to dance to my own drum.

GROSSET & DUNLAP
Published by the Penguin Group
Penguin Group (USA) LLC, 375 Hudson Street, New York, New York 10014, USA

USA | Canada | UK | Ireland | Australia | New Zealand | India | South Africa | China

penguin.com
A Penguin Random House Company

Text copyright © 2014 by GDL Foods, Inc. Illustrations copyright © 2014 by Francesca Gambatesa. All rights reserved.
Published by Grosset & Dunlap, a division of Penguin Young Readers Group, 345 Hudson Street, New York, New York 10014.
GROSSET & DUNLAP is a trademark of Penguin Group (USA) LLC. Printed in the USA.

Library of Congress Cataloging-in-Publication Data is available.

ISBN 978-0-448-46259-2 (pbk)   10 9 8 7 6 5 4 3 2
ISBN 978-0-448-48049-7 (hc)   10 9 8 7 6 5 4 3 2

family—Mom, Dad, Alfie, Emilia, and their great-aunt Donatella—had just finished their picnic lunch. It was a lazy Saturday afternoon in the park, and the sun was shining bright.

"What a great afternoon," Dad said to Mom.

"And don't forget the party we have to look forward to tonight," Mom reminded him.

Alfie and Emilia's parents were going out to celebrate a friend's birthday. Alfie and Emilia would stay home with Zia, which was always fun. They never knew what kind of adventure Zia might cook up for them. So far, Zia's magical recipes had transported them to Naples, Paris, and Hong Kong!

Alfie and Emilia collapsed onto the blanket after their latest round of Frisbee. Mom leaned back on her hands and said, "*Che bello*. We should do this more often."

Dad put down his paper. "What we need to do is plan that family *viaggio*: the vacation we keep talking about."

"That's a wonderful idea," Zia Donatella said,

adjusting her round black sunglasses. Mom and Dad were always busy with work and didn't take enough time to relax. The family hadn't been on a vacation together in years.

"Yes!" Mom said. "Where should we go?"

Alfie and Emilia exchanged a glance. Little did their parents know, they'd been to a few cities recently, but they were always up for discovering somewhere new.

"We could go to Japan," Alfie said.

"Yeah, Japan," Emilia quickly agreed. "Or maybe Australia."

"Sweden!"

"France!" Emilia added.

"But we've already been to P—" Alfie started to say. Zia cleared her throat and touched the brightly colored stone necklace she always wore.

"How about Mongolia?" Alfie quickly changed directions.

Mom laughed. "Sounds exciting, but just what kind of

family vacation do you think we're taking?"

"An adventurous one!" Alfie said, his eyes sparkling with excitement.

"Someplace like Arizona sounds adventurous to me," Dad said.

"Arizona?!" Alfie responded.

"Yeah, Arizona. You know, desert landscapes, Lake Havasu, a little something called the Grand Canyon!" Dad replied.

"I guess." Alfie shrugged.

"Or we could go mountain biking in the Rocky Mountains," Dad said.

"That's a good idea," Mom said. "You take your bike up on the ski lift and then ride down the mountain. Doesn't that sound fun?"

Alfie had to agree that sounded pretty cool. But still . . . there were so many places in the world to see. He was hoping his parents would take them somewhere outside the United States.

"How about," Alfie began, "instead of mountain biking in the Rockies, we do it in the Alps?"

"Yeah," Emilia said. "The Swiss Alps!"

"We're happy you're both so interested in world travel," said Mom. "But for now, we'll stay a bit closer to home. Like Washington, DC. There's so much great history there."

Emilia perked up. She loved history as much as Alfie loved maps.

"Hey, Emilia. You know what place has tons of history?" Alfie asked. "Greece! We could go see the Acropolis of Athens. Right?" he said to his parents.

"Zia," Mom said, shaking her head. "What are we going to do with these two?"

Zia smiled. "I think there are so many wonderful places in America to see that it'd be hard to see them all in one lifetime. But we can start trying."

"*Brava!*" Dad said. "Zia's got the right attitude."

Mom began packing the leftover pasta salad, grilled

vegetables, and flatbread into their picnic basket. "Well, let's keep thinking about where we might want to go. But for now, your dad and I need to get home so we can get ready for our evening out. What have you got planned for tonight, Zia?" she asked.

Alfie and Emilia helped Zia fold up the picnic blanket. "Oh, I'm sure we'll find something fun to do," Zia said. "Maybe something in the kitchen?" She sneaked a quick wink at Alfie and Emilia.

"Yes!" Alfie and Emilia said at once. There weren't many things they loved more than being in the kitchen with Zia Donatella. Hearing her tell stories about her travels was better than any movie or video game. Because when Zia cooked, she always took them someplace special.

Chapter 2

Mom was all dressed up when she walked into the living room. She fastened a bracelet around her wrist.

"Mom, you look nice," Emilia said, looking up from where she sat on the floor with Alfie and Zia. They were huddled around the coffee table, working on a puzzle.

"*Grazie, amore.* Thank you, love," Mom said. "So, Zia, did you say you're going to cook dinner or you're going out?"

Zia Donatella frowned at Mom.

"*Cucina,*" Mom said. "You'll cook. Of course."

"I have a plan for tonight that I think the kids are going to love," Zia said. "Something *interessante*, a little interesting, to help them see how wonderful it is right

here in their own backyard. Ha! Found one," she said,
locking a puzzle piece into place.

Alfio propped his elbow on the table and rested his
chin in his hand. He and Emilia never knew when one
of Zia's magical recipes might send them to a new place.
They were always ready to meet new friends and taste
amazing new foods. But it sounded like tonight wouldn't
be one of those nights.

Dad came into the living room wrestling with his tie.
"Whatever you decide to do, have fun tonight," he said.

"And you kids try to behave yourselves," Mom added as she fixed Dad's tie for him.

"We'll find some kind of trouble to get into, don't worry." Zia smiled.

Mom and Dad kissed Alfie and Emilia on their heads and left for the party.

"Now then," Zia said, getting up from the floor. "Time to start dinner."

"Already?" Alfie looked at the clock. "It's kind of early."

"Some dishes take time," Zia said. "Like the one I want us to make tonight."

Emilia and Alfie followed Zia into the kitchen. "What can we do to help?" Emilia asked.

"We can start with the holy trinity," Zia said.

"What's that?"

"For this dish, it's three things: onion, celery, and bell pepper. They all need to be diced."

"I'm on it." Emilia slid over to the fridge in her polka-dot socks. She carried the ingredients back to the cutting board, where Zia watched her chop up the vegetables.

"Careful now," Zia said. "Take your time, and keep those fingers out of the way."

"I will," Emilia said, concentrating.

"While she's doing that, we can start on a key part of the dish," Zia told Alfie. "The roux."

"I'm ready," Alfie said. He was happy to handle the important stuff and leave the dicing to Emilia.

"To make the roux we need equal parts butter and flour," Zia said, pulling out a heavy stockpot and a stick of butter. "Alfredo, will you get the flour from the pantry?"

"Sure," Alfie said.

"What's *roo*, anyway?" Emilia asked, keeping her eyes on the cutting board.

"Roux, spelled *r-o-u-x*, is a special base sauce," Zia said.

"Sounds French," Emilia said, stopping to look at Alfie. He knew what that look meant. Maybe they were going back to Paris, or to somewhere else in France?

Zia nodded. "Very good."

"What else?" Alfie asked, setting the flour on the counter.

"That's it for now." Zia waited until the pot was hot, then she added the butter and swirled it around. "Keep watching the butter until it's melted. Then we're ready to go."

Once the melted butter had coated the bottom of the pot, Zia slowly began to sprinkle in the flour and whisked them together. "We do this until we get the color and thickness we want. Here you go, Alfredo," she said, handing him the whisk and the rest of the flour.

"You haven't told us what we're making," Alfie said as he whisked. Soon the flour and butter started to darken into a creamy mixture the color of peanut butter.

"We need one other very important ingredient,"

Zia said, walking over to the fridge. She brought a large sausage link over to Emilia's cutting board. "Slice this andouille sausage into coins, about this thick." She demonstrated the first slice.

"*An-dooey*," Alfie repeated. "But what is the dish?" He couldn't stand not knowing what they were cooking!

"We're making an authentic New Orleans, Louisiana–style gumbo," said Zia.

"New Orleans?" Alfie asked as he whisked and whisked. His right arm was getting tired so he switched to his left. "Then why does it sound French?"

"Because it was the French who originally founded the city," Zia said. "Then the Spanish took it over, then the French took it back, and then the Americans bought it during a thing called . . ."

"The Louisiana Purchase!" Emilia chimed in.

"That's right!" Zia said.

Alfie switched back to whisking with his right arm and shook out his left. He eyed Emilia's chopping station enviously. "How do you know so much about New Orleans's history?" he asked Zia.

"Well, I don't just eat my way through cities," she said. "It's important to know a little history about the places you visit, too."

"And before the French and Spanish lived in New Orleans, the Native Americans lived there," Emilia said. "They didn't call it New Orleans, though."

"*Brava!*" said Zia. "Very good. And all those different cultures, along with a rich history of African American traditions, helped influence the food that's eaten there today. How's that roux coming along?" Zia looked in Alfie's pot. The mixture was now the color of milk chocolate. "*Perfetto!* That's perfect. Time to bring all the ingredients together. Emilia, put the holy trinity in the pot here. Alfie, keep stirring."

Emilia brought the onion, celery, and pepper to Zia and pulled up a kitchen stool to watch. Zia handed Alfie a wooden spoon to replace his whisk. Alfie sighed and switched arms again. *Since when did cooking become such hard work?*

Next Zia slid the sausage into the pot. "Some people add chicken and shrimp or other seafood to their gumbo, but I like mine simple with just sausage. It adds a perfect smoky flavor."

"When were you in New Orleans, Zia?" Emilia asked.

"Yeah, and what was it like?" Alfie added.

"New Orleans is like no other place in the US *or* the world," Zia said. "The food is so unique, it can't be found anywhere else. And the music! Music is as important to the city as food. When I was there, goodness, it was ages ago now, I met a trumpet player who played jazz just like he made his gumbo—full of warmth and soulfulness. We met his friends and danced on a balcony overlooking Bourbon Street. I don't think I've ever had so much energy in my life. We danced all night!"

"Sounds like one big party!" Alfie said.

"The city loves any reason to celebrate, that's for

sure," said Zia. "But they also love taking their time about things—like their gumbo. Almost time to add the spices. But keep stirring!"

Alfie switched arms yet again, not wanting to admit how tired he was.

Zia slowly added chicken broth to the mixture. "And now for the spices," she said. "A little thyme, two bay leaves, a pinch of salt, some fresh garlic, a dash of cayenne pepper for kick. Stir it all together, Alfie." Alfie hadn't stopped stirring for what seemed like an hour! "And of course, the ingredient my trumpeter friend showed me: ground sassafras leaves. This is also called *filé* powder or gumbo *filé*. Just a little goes into the pot and *violà!*"

"Time to eat?" Alfie asked. All that stirring had made him hungry!

"Not yet," Zia said. "The longer it simmers, the better the flavor. Oh—you can stop stirring now."

Alfie happily stepped away from the stove.

While the gumbo simmered, Zia started cooking some

white rice. Then she put on some music.

"What kind of music is this?" Emilia asked.

"This is jazz. Jazz was born in New Orleans, just like this gumbo."

Alfie picked up two wooden spoons and tapped the handles against the counter in rhythm to the music. He had just started learning to play the drums. Maybe he could be a jazz drummer!

Zia stirred the gumbo and let the steam drift over her face. "Mmmm," she said. "I think it's ready." She took two bowls from the cupboard and added a scoop of rice to the bottom of each. Then she ladled a cup of gumbo over the top of the rice.

"Aren't you eating, too, Zia?" Emilia asked.

She smiled. "I will in a minute. I want you two to try it first."

Zia set the bowls in front of Alfie and Emilia and leaned on the counter. "We eat with our eyes first. See how hearty and comforting that looks, but festive, too, with the bursts of pepper," she said. "That's what comes to mind when I think of New Orleans. Comfort food. And everyone is so friendly and laid-back—just like the food. Now, smell."

Alfie put his nose close to the bowl. The gumbo smelled rich and spicy.

"One thing's for sure," said Zia. "You'll never be hungry when you go to New Orleans! Just take one bite and you'll understand."

Alfie and Emilia lifted their spoons and blew on the hot gumbo. They took a bite at the same time. The sauce was soupy and coated Alfie's mouth in an explosion of flavors and spices—hot but not too spicy. The onions, celery, and pepper had softened and gave extra flavor to everything. Alfie's favorite part was the andouille sausage. Zia was right—it had a smoky flavor and perfect chewiness all on its own.

"This is amazing," Alfie said. He scooped up another big bite, this time making sure to get some rice on his spoon. "It's spicy, but I like it."

"Me too," Emilia said. "And with this music, I feel like I'm there!"

"Oh, you should see the bands that play!" Zia said. "Leading wedding parties right down the middle of the street—everyone dancing, including people just passing by. New Orleans knows how to throw a party. And everything is a celebration, but especially the food. A city so diverse deserves to celebrate every day."

Alfie was all for celebrating. He could see the dancing, hear the music, and even feel the heat of the city itself, all right there in his bowl of gumbo. Just when he decided that maybe New Orleans would be a great place to visit, he got that feeling in the pit of his stomach that told him to hold on—one of Zia's adventures was coming up . . .

Chapter 3

Whenever Alfie and Emilia started a new adventure, there was always a moment of confusion while Alfie waited for his senses to adjust. In Hong Kong he'd arrived in the middle of a busy sidewalk. This time, he was in the dark—literally. But he could hear music: loud horns, rippling piano, steady drums. It sounded kind of like the jazz they had just been listening to with Zia Donatella, but even more lively.

As his eyes adjusted, he reached out for Emilia's hand, relieved to know she was there, too. She always was, but Alfie was still getting used to these trips of Zia's, and he never knew what to expect.

Just then, someone rushed by carrying a tray full of steaming-hot food. Alfie and Emilia stepped aside and realized they were in a doorway looking out into some sort of club. Small round tables with little lamps packed the dark space. Many of the tables were empty, but there were a few people dotted around the room, and they all faced the stage. Hot lights lit up five musicians who played the music with their whole bodies, leaning into the piano and drums, swinging their horns, and tapping their feet.

"New Orleans!" Emilia said.

"I think so," Alfie said. He could still feel the heat of Zia's gumbo on his tongue.

"They look young." Emilia pointed to the band. She had to raise her voice to be heard over the wail of the trumpet, which was being played by a boy who looked about their age. The drummer seemed to be their parents' age, but most of the band were older teenagers or maybe in their early twenties. "And there's a girl!" Emilia added.

Sure enough, a girl in cut-off jeans and a black fedora was playing the clarinet.

"I can't wait to meet them," Emilia said. "We're going to meet them, right?"

"Yeah, I guess," Alfie said. They always met someone their own ages when Zia sent them on an adventure, so he figured New Orleans would be no different.

When one song made its way into the next, the piano player hollered for applause. He seemed to be the leader of the band. When that song was over, they immediately rolled into the next one. This one was about cornbread and butter beans, and it was sung by the piano player. He had a strong, thick voice, and people clapped along as he performed.

"They even *sing* about food here," Alfie said. Emilia nodded and bobbed her head to the music. In the middle of this song, each one of the musicians took a little solo. Alfie paid extra attention to the drummer's fast beats, tapping his fingers against his legs in rhythm. The crowd

applauded after each solo, and Alfie and Emilia joined in.

"They're really good!" Emilia said.

Soon, the music came to an end, and the piano player said, "Thank you! We are the La Salle Royale Band! Come back and see us real soon. Good night!"

"Come on, let's go meet them!" Emilia said, leading the way to the side of the stage.

"What are we going to say?" Alfie asked his sister.

Emilia thought for a moment. "We can say we're visiting New Orleans with our school. And that we got separated from them or something."

"No," Alfie said. "Then they might try to help us find our group or take us to the police station."

"True," Emilia said, still thinking.

"They're pretty good, aren't they?" A boy about fifteen or sixteen appeared next to Alfie and nodded toward the stage.

"Yeah, they were great!" Alfie said.

"I guess I'm a little biased since they *are* my family." The boy laughed. "I'm Rex," he said.

"I'm Alfie." He shook Rex's hand. "And this is my sister, Emilia."

"Nice to meet you," Rex said. He glanced toward the front of the stage and furrowed his brow. Alfie followed Rex's gaze. The piano player was talking to an older man. Alfie could tell Rex was straining to hear their conversation. Alfie tried to listen, too.

"Sorry, Virgil," the older man said. "We all need to make money."

"We just need a little more time," the young man, Virgil, said.

"As I told your parents, I can give you till the end of the month," the man said. "But that's the best I can do." He put his hand on Virgil's shoulder. "You know how much I love your family, and we all miss Mama Minnie, but . . . if things don't pick up, there's nothing more I can do." Virgil looked down and nodded.

Rex turned back to Emilia and Alfie, a smile slowly returning to his face. "Come on. I'll introduce you to my family!"

Alfie and Emilia grinned. Their adventure was beginning.

Chapter 4

"Nanette!" Rex called to the girl who'd been playing clarinet. "Come meet Alfie and Emilia."

Nanette snapped her clarinet case closed and hopped down from the stage, holding her hat as she jumped. "Hi!" she said.

"That was really great!" Emilia gushed. "We loved your songs."

"Thank you." Nanette looked pleased. "You guys here for Jazz Fest?"

"Uh, yeah. Yes, Jazz Fest!" Alfie said without thinking.

"We're on a school field trip," Emilia chimed in.

Alfie elbowed Emilia's side and gave her a look.

He thought they'd decided not to use that story. The last thing he wanted was to end up on the evening news or something. "But our aunt lives here," he added quickly.

"Nice," Nanette said.

"Are those *all* your brothers?" Emilia asked, gesturing to the stage.

"All except for the drummer," Nanette replied. "He's a family friend. But the other three are. Four in all, including Rex. Lucky me, right?"

Just then, the trumpet player hopped down next to Nanette and Rex. Nanette pulled him under her arm and rubbed his head. "But they're not so bad. Especially this guy. This is my little brother, Theodore. He's eleven."

"It's Teddy," the boy said, patting his hair. "And I just turned twelve. Nanette thinks she's a big shot now that she's thirteen."

Alfie nodded and smirked. "My sister's one year older, too. I know the feeling." He liked Teddy already—they both had shortened nicknames and slightly older, slightly annoying sisters.

"This is Alfie and Emilia," Rex said.

"You guys gonna eat dinner with us?" Teddy asked.

Alfie and Emilia looked at each other.

"Or is your school group waiting for you?" Nanette asked, glancing around the club. "Where *is* your school group?"

"Oh, they already left," Alfie said. "Our school trip is done, but we're staying with our aunt this weekend, and she knows where we are." He hoped he sounded convincing. Zia Donatella *did* know where they were . . . kind of.

"Well, if nobody's waiting for you, you're welcome to join us. We were just about to head back to the kitchen," Nanette said.

"Sure, if that's okay," Emilia said.

"Have you had real New Orleans–style food yet?" Rex asked.

"Not really," Alfie said. "We're definitely ready to try it. We're hoping to eat our way through New Orleans!"

"You came to the right place, or the right family, then," Rex said, leading the way to the kitchen.

Alfie and Emilia smiled at each other. Everything was going perfectly so far.

Chapter 5

Alfie and Emilia followed their new friends past the doorway where they first arrived and through a swinging door into the kitchen. There was a long rectangular table in the corner near the dish-washing station. It was already piled high with plates of food.

"Thanks, Gus!" Rex called to one of the cooks. The man nodded and waved a metal serving spoon.

"The cooks always save leftovers for us," Nanette told Alfie and Emilia. Alfie wasn't exactly sure what all the food was, but it looked—and smelled—great.

As if reading his mind, Rex started pointing out all the dishes. "We've got blackened catfish, red beans and rice, collard greens, and cornbread."

Just then the two older brothers burst through the kitchen door.

"We have guests," Rex told them. "Alfie and Emilia are in town for Jazz Fest, and they want to eat their way through the city."

"Welcome to New Orleans. I'm Jules," said the young man who played the trombone. He grabbed a piece of cornbread and stuffed half of it into his mouth.

"Short for Julian," Teddy added. "He's nineteen, but he acts like he's the youngest."

"Not true," Jules said through the cornbread. "It's just that Virgil here is so good at being the old man that I don't dare take the honor away from him."

Virgil gave a half smile, but stayed focused on dishing his plate. Alfie thought he still looked upset from his conversation in front of the stage.

"Virgil plays piano and also writes some of our songs," Teddy said.

"What instrument do you play?" Emilia asked Rex.

Rex shook his head and finished chewing. "I don't," he said. "I tried saxophone like our mom, then I tried drums like our dad, but I just never really got into anything."

"Your parents are musicians, too?" Alfie asked.

"Yep," Nanette said. "They've got a gig on a riverboat right now. Their friend Sam fills in on drums whenever they're gone."

"Where is Sam?" Jules asked. "He's not eating with us tonight?"

"Nope," Teddy said. "He wanted to catch the end of the Trickster Trio's set."

Alfie took a bite of catfish. It was buttery on the inside and crispy on the outside. The thick seasoning coated his tongue with several flavors at once—peppery, sweet, and spicy.

"So, what do you think of our place?" Teddy said, gesturing around the kitchen.

"This is your place?" Alfie asked. He had assumed they just played here.

"Yep. Didn't you notice our name on the outside of the building when you came in?"

Alfie just nodded. He couldn't tell them they hadn't exactly come in through the front door ...

"It's also our band name and our last name," said Teddy. "La Salle Royale is the best club in town, serving the best food. Well, it used to be the best ..."

"Used to be?" Emilia asked, dishing up a helping of collard greens.

A sad look came over Teddy's face. "Our grandmother passed away suddenly last year. She was the cook in the family, and she's the one who really made a name for us in New Orleans. The band is great and all, but her cooking was really amazing."

"I'm sorry about your grandmother," Emilia said.

"We miss her so much," Nanette said. "Our parents travel a lot with their riverboat gigs, and Mama Minnie was always the one who looked after us, especially when we were younger. Now Virgil's stuck with the job."

"Ah, y'all are pretty easy to deal with," Virgil said.

"Virgil doesn't get enough credit," said Jules. "Not only does he have to look after the family, but he has to deal with Charlie when Mom and Dad are gone."

"Who's Charlie?" Alfie asked. He scooped up a heap of red beans and rice. It had a creamy, slightly spicy taste that warmed him all the way down to his toes. Zia was right—this was comfort food.

"Charlie owns this building," Virgil said. "We lease the space for our club from him."

"No offense to Gus or anything, but no one can cook like Mama Minnie did," Nanette said. "So, since she passed away, things just haven't been the same here."

Alfie thought about all the empty tables he saw when they first arrived.

"We'll be fine," Virgil said. "We always are."

Alfie stabbed a bite of collard greens with his fork. "Are her recipes hard to follow or something?" The greens were salty and surprisingly juicy, with bits of

bacon adding a chewy texture. It tasted great!

"Following a recipe isn't necessarily the problem," Teddy said. "If you give three trumpet players the same sheet of music and ask them to play, you'll hear three different versions of the same song. Same with cooking— that's what Mama Minnie used to say. But following a recipe doesn't matter, because she never wrote anything down. No one will ever know what made her red beans and rice so great." He looked down at his plate.

"Well, we've got to figure out some way to bring people back to the club," said Virgil. "If we can't . . . good-bye La Salle Royale."

"I can't even think about our place becoming a Cozy Creole." Nanette shook her head.

"What's a Cozy Creole?" Alfie asked. He was already on his second piece of cornbread. He used the crumbly, buttery bread to scoop up the rest of the beans and rice on his plate. He couldn't help himself. He glanced at Emilia, expecting her to tell him to slow down, but she was just as busy finishing off her piece of catfish. It was hard to imagine feeling disappointed about this food. Alfie thought it was amazing!

"Cozy Creole is a chain restaurant. Charlie plans on leasing the space to them if things don't pick up," Rex said. "The food is nothing close to what Mama Minnie used to make. Hers was the real deal." Rex pushed his plate away and sighed. "If only *I'd* started writing her recipes down when she was teaching me to cook. I just didn't expect her not to be around..."

Everyone nodded in quiet agreement.

"Finish up, y'all," Virgil said, breaking the silence. "We need to get home."

"Yeah, your aunt's probably wondering where you are," Rex said to Alfie and Emilia. "You okay to get to her place on your own? Where does she live?"

Alfie hadn't thought this far ahead. Luckily, Emilia spoke up.

"We can get there," she said. "She's not home right now—she works late hours. But, um, she'll be there later."

"Will you guys be okay on your own?" Virgil asked.

"Yeah, it's not a big deal," Alfie said, trying to sound casual. But he was already wondering where they might go.

"Because you're welcome to come to our house until she gets home," Virgil said.

"Maybe they should just stay the night since it's

already kind of late?" Teddy said.

"Well, if it's okay with their aunt," said Virgil. "Honestly, I'd rather you stay with us than be on your own half the night."

"Maybe we can call her and ask if it's okay?" Emilia said to Alfie, giving him a look.

"Yeah, I'll call her," Alfie said.

"You can use the phone on the wall," Teddy said.

Alfie wasn't sure what he was going to do!

He picked up the receiver and kept his back to the table as he punched in a bunch of random numbers. He pressed the "disconnect" bar just as someone actually said "hello." Then he started talking.

"Hello! Aunt Donatella. Yeah, it's Alfie. Um, we're at La Salle Royale and we just—you know the place? Yeah, it's awesome. So, since you're working late,

Virgil La Salle said we could crash with them tonight. Is that okay? Great! Okay, we'll see you tomorrow then."

Suddenly, Virgil was standing behind Alfie. "Can I talk to her?" he asked.

"Okay. Thanks, Aunt Donatella. Bye!" Alfie quickly hung up the phone. "Sorry, what'd you say?"

Virgil frowned and said, "I just wanted to talk to her, give her our address and everything. Want to call her back?"

"Nah, she's cool," Alfie said, walking back to the table.

"So, it's set!" Teddy said. "You're staying with the La Salle Royale Band!"

Chapter 6

The walk to the La Salle family house took them along the lively streets of the French Quarter. Alfie loved the rows of beautiful buildings with decorative wrought iron balconies. He tried to picture Zia Donatella dancing all night on one of them.

They passed by street musicians and dancers with taps on the bottoms of their shoes. Large crowds had gathered to watch them all perform. People were clapping and hollering and really getting into the music. One of the dancers, who was taking a break just outside the circle, waved as they passed. "Hey, Virgil!" he called out. "Happy Jazz Fest!"

It was hard for Alfie to imagine a scene like that in his town. Zia Donatella was right—there was plenty of adventure to be had even in his own country! As they continued through the city, the noise of people and music fell away to a quiet residential vibe. They entered the La Salles' neighborhood, passing Washington Square Park.

Rex gestured to the park. "After Hurricane Katrina, we helped set up a free community kitchen here. Luckily our neighborhood wasn't hit as bad as a lot of the others, so we wanted to help out however we could. Mama Minnie worked night and day cooking for people out here. Virgil and Jules helped serve the food."

Alfie nodded. "That's really nice." He didn't really remember Hurricane Katrina, but they definitely had learned about it in school.

They kept walking past a big four-lane street with fresh green grass running down the center.

"Alfie, look," Emilia said, pointing to the street sign. "It's called Elysian Fields Avenue. It kind of reminds me of that big, famous street in Paris—Champs-Élysées. Am I crazy?"

"Probably," Alfie teased.

"No, she's right," Nanette chimed in. "It's not as fancy here, but this street is named after the one in Paris. Even the name of our neighborhood, Faubourg Marigny, is French. *Faubourg* means *suburb* and Marigny is the name of a rich Creole man who settled here a long, long time ago. New Orleans has lots of cool history, if you're into things like that."

"I definitely am!" Emilia beamed.

They crossed Elysian Fields, and right on the corner at Dauphine Street was the La Salle home. It was a big two-story white house with an upper balcony and a huge front porch. Virgil unlocked the door and let them all in.

Wide-plank wooden floorboards creaked under their feet as they walked into the foyer. A curving staircase led up to the second floor. Alfie thought it looked like something out of an old movie. There were family pictures on every wall and surface—including on an upright piano in the living room, which led into a huge kitchen.

Virgil dropped his bag next to the piano, and sheets of music spilled out onto the floor. He sat down and began to play quietly, despite having just spent the entire evening performing.

"Wow, this place is awesome!" Alfie said.

"Yeah," Emilia agreed. "It's so pretty. And so big!"

"We're a big family," said Rex. "Mama Minnie lived here with us. This kitchen was her pride and joy. Now I can barely keep everybody's music out of here."

Alfie could see what Rex meant. Instrument parts, music stands, band flyers, and sheet music were scattered everywhere. "Who cooks in here now?"

"Our parents cook when we're not eating at the club," Rex said. "And whatever I can remember from Mama Minnie's recipes I try to re-create here. It's hard, though. She was just such a natural."

Virgil appeared in the doorway. "Okay, you two and you two," he said, gesturing to Teddy, Nanette, Alfie, and Emilia. "Time for bed."

"But they just got here," Teddy argued.

"You can show them everything tomorrow," Virgil said, looking tired. "For now, get them settled in the extra room and make sure they have everything they need."

"Thanks for letting us stay," Alfie said.

"No worries," said Virgil.

"Come on, I'll show you up," Teddy said, leading the way upstairs with Nanette right behind him.

Teddy took them down a long hall to a room at the end. Alfie studied the walls of the hallway as they walked. They were covered in family portraits as well as pictures of the kids and their parents playing onstage in front of huge crowds.

Their room had a window in the center with twin beds on either side. Each bed had a thick quilt across it. Nanette reappeared with a pile of stuff. "Here are some T-shirts and shorts you can wear to bed. And some clothes for tomorrow that should fit."

"Thanks," Emilia said, taking the pile.

"See you in the morning," Teddy said.

Alfie closed the door behind Teddy and flopped down on the bed facing Emilia. He grinned as the soft sound of Virgil's piano playing floated up to the room. "Here we go again," he said.

Chapter 7

Alfie woke up to sunlight streaming through the thin curtains. Emilia's bed was empty, and he heard voices downstairs. Music from the piano still hung in the air, as if Virgil hadn't stopped playing all night. More importantly, Alfie smelled breakfast cooking. He quickly dressed in the clothes Nanette had given him: a pair of jeans, a short-sleeved button-down shirt, a bow tie, and a funny flat-topped straw hat. Luckily, he'd learned to tie a bow tie for their uncle's wedding last year. He felt a little silly putting on it and the hat, but he didn't want to disappoint Nanette.

"Good morning," Alfie said as his foot touched the bottom step.

"Good morning, little man." Virgil glanced up from the piano.

"Did you play all night?" Alfie asked, only half joking.

"Nah, I just got up," he said. "I'm working on a new song for the band."

"Well, I like what I've heard so far," Alfie told him before he headed into the kitchen.

Rex and Emilia were at the stove. Rex whisked something in a heavy-bottomed pot. Emilia stirred scrambled eggs in a pan over low heat while keeping an eye on sausage frying in another pan. Emilia wore a red shirt, rolled-up jeans, and a hair band with a matching bright red flower on it.

"You're just in time," said Rex. "Breakfast is almost ready." He removed the pot from the burner, added some butter, and continued stirring.

"Good, we're starving!" Teddy and Nanette hurried into the kitchen.

Alfie watched Rex as he worked. "Seems like you know what you're doing in the kitchen," he told Rex.

"Making eggs and grits isn't cooking. Not really," Rex said. He added a handful of grated cheese to the pot. "I think we were all born knowing how to cook this. Too easy."

"I think the eggs are ready," Emilia said, turning off her burner. "And the sausage, too."

"Perfect timing," Rex said. "A little more cheese and

the grits should be good to go. Everyone get a plate!"

Virgil and Jules appeared at the edge of the kitchen counter.

Alfie grabbed a stack of plates from on top of a bunch of Jazz Fest flyers and handed them out to everyone. He added a scoop each of eggs and grits to his plate and picked up a piece of sausage. The sausage looked like the andouille they'd used in the gumbo. It was quickly becoming one of Alfie's favorites. "I've never had grits before," he said as he moved over to the big dining-room table to sit down.

"You're going to love them," Rex said. "They're ground cornmeal with a good helping of butter and cheese."

"Everything tastes better with butter and cheese, if you ask me," Teddy said, taking a seat next to Alfie.

Alfie took a bite. The grits were super buttery and creamy, and the cheese gave them an extra bit of rich flavor. "Wow," he said, scooping up another forkful. "They're so good."

"The grits go perfectly with the eggs and sausage," Emilia added.

"Yeah, nice work," Jules said, shoving a big bite into his mouth.

Alfie looked around the room as he ate his delicious breakfast. "You have a lot of pictures," he remarked, noticing even more in the morning light than he had the night before.

"Yeah," said Teddy. "Mom and Dad love having lots of memories all around us. Mom says that way we can see how great a life we're living and not take anything for granted."

"Plus it's fun to see things they did before we were born," said Nanette. "Like that picture over there of them playing for the president back in the day." Nanette motioned to a framed photo on the open center shelf of the china cabinet.

Alfie got up and walked over to get a closer look. He picked up the frame. In the photo, their mom stood smiling and holding a microphone while their dad held his drumsticks and shook the former president's hand.

"That's so cool!" Alfie said. He was just about to set the photo down when something slid out of the back of the frame and onto the floor. It was another photo—a black-and-white one, even older than the one in the frame. Alfie picked up the picture. Two women were posed side by side, smiling. "What's this?" he asked.

Nanette got a curious look on her face. "Not sure. Pass it here for a second." Nanette took the photo and her eyes widened in surprise. "That's our Mama Minnie when she was young! I've never seen this picture before. Guys, look at this!"

Rex, Virgil, Jules, and Teddy all gathered around Nanette at the table. They peered down at the photograph.

"She's so young!" Teddy said. "Who's that standing next to her?"

Virgil took the photo from Nanette. "I don't know who that other woman is," he said. "But it looks like they're standing in front of Mr. Picard's grocery."

Jules peered over Virgil's shoulder. "What's she holding in her hand? Does that say 'cookbook' on the front?"

Rex grabbed the photo from Virgil and studied it closely. "I think it does!"

"No way," Teddy said. "Let me see."

Rex passed him the photo. "Hey, it does."

"Told'ya," Rex said.

"But whose cookbook?" Teddy asked.

"Probably your Mama Minnie's, right?" Emilia asked.

"But I thought she never wrote anything down," Rex said. "And she never said anything about a cookbook."

"It could be the other woman's recipes," Virgil said. "People always wanted to have their picture taken with Mama Minnie."

"That grocery store is still around," Jules added. "It's over on Basin Street in the French Quarter. I remember meeting Mr. Picard years ago."

"We could go!" Teddy said. "Let's go see Mr. Picard!"

"And then what?" Virgil asked. "What if Mr. Picard's not around anymore?"

Teddy shrugged. "Maybe he knows who this other woman is. And maybe that woman knows if Mama Minnie had a recipe book."

"Just think," Emilia said. "If you had Mama Minnie's recipes, you could use them again in this great big kitchen."

"And at La Salle Royale," Alfie added, feeling excited.

"True," Virgil said thoughtfully.

"We *have* to go to the market and talk to Mr. Picard!" Teddy said. "If we can find out who that woman is, maybe we can talk to her. Even if she doesn't know about the cookbook, maybe she can tell us stories about Mama Minnie. I'd be happy with that."

Virgil's face softened. Alfie could see that they all missed their grandmother very much. "Okay," Virgil said. "Go talk to Mr. Picard. I guess it can't hurt."

"Yes!" Teddy cheered. "Come on, Alfie and Emilia, let's get going!" Alfie felt a rush of excitement along with him.

"I'm coming, too!" Nanette said, pushing back from her chair.

"Make sure you're back in time for us to head to the club together," Virgil said. "And don't forget, Theodore— it's your turn to pick up dinner. You got money?"

"Yep!" Teddy patted his pants pocket.

Rex started cleaning up.

Teddy already was racing toward the front door with Nanette behind him, grabbing her hat as she went.

"And make sure Alfie and Emilia's aunt doesn't mind!" Virgil called out after them.

Aunt, schmant, Alfie thought. They had a mystery to solve!

Chapter 8

The foursome headed out the door. The late-morning sun was already bright and hot.

"Y'all are lucky Jazz Fest is in the spring and not the summer," Nanette said. "It gets even hotter and more humid in July and August."

Alfie thought it was pretty hot already, and he could definitely feel a stickiness in the air as they walked. He got a better sense of the neighborhood seeing it in the light of day. The La Salle house was one of a few big two-story homes; most were long one-story houses. Some were painted fun, bright colors like purple or blue. And almost all of them had porches where some people sat outside drinking coffee, enjoying their morning.

Soon they were back in the French Quarter with its elegant buildings and fancy balconies. Bright flowers hung from pots below the balconies and swayed in the breeze.

"Let's walk into the park for a minute," Nanette said.

They crossed Rampart Street and headed through a lightbulb-covered arch into Louis Armstrong Park.

"Maybe you already learned this from your school tour, but Louis Armstrong is, like, the most famous musician ever born or raised in New Orleans," Teddy said proudly. "He played the trumpet, just like me."

"And Congo Square," Nanette said, motioning to their left, "is where Jazz Fest first started when our parents were young. It was called Beauregard Square back then."

"And your parents taught you all to play?" Alfie asked.

"Yep," said Teddy. "It was pretty easy to pick up—we grew up surrounded by music with our parents and their friends. Learning to read and play music was as normal as learning to read a book."

"Music and food—that's what we've grown up on,"
Nanette added. "I remember Mama Minnie cooking up
fried chicken and biscuits while Mom and Dad played in the
living room. The smells and sounds just filled up the house."

Alfie smiled. He thought about how nice it had been to
have Zia Donatella's cooking fill their house with yummy
smells, too. As much as he used to love pizza from Presto
Pesto, it just didn't smell the same as Zia's cooking.

They wove through the park and walked out onto
Basin Street. A few blocks later, Alfie spotted Picard's
Produce and More. Stands filled with colorful rows of
fruits and vegetables stood outside on the sidewalk.

"Let's hope Mr. Picard is here," Teddy said.

"And that he knows something about Mama Minnie or
the other woman in the picture," Nanette added.

The door chimed when Teddy pulled it open. Inside,
there were even more rows of fruits and veggies lining the
walls. And in front stood giant barrels full of more kinds
of nuts than Alfie had ever seen.

"Hello!" A voice called from the back of the store. "Be right there!" Alfie couldn't see anyone past the tightly packed shelves.

A man made his way up the narrow aisle, pushing aside a box as he went. "Anything I can help you with?" he asked. He was old, but he looked strong—probably from moving all those big barrels around every day, Alfie thought

"Actually, we're looking for Mr. Picard," Teddy said.

The man strolled around to the other side of the front counter. "Well, you found him!" he said. "What can I do for ya?"

"We were hoping you might be able to help us," Teddy said, stepping forward and sliding the photograph across the counter. "Do you know this woman?"

As soon as he picked up the photo, happiness spread across his wrinkled face. "Well, look at that! Miss Minnie La Salle!"

"You knew Mama Minnie?" Nanette asked.

"Sure I did!" Mr. Picard said. "She used to come in here every week when she was a young 'un to buy pecans. And you must be her grandchildren." He motioned to the La Salle kids.

"I'm Nanette, and this is Teddy," she said.

Mr. Picard looked pleased to see them. "Minnie used to bring Virgil and Julian in here when they were young. And now they're all grown up! And I've seen y'all play at La Salle Royale! Such a talented family." The pleasure faded from Mr. Picard's face. "Just hasn't been the same down there without Minnie and her cooking, though, has it?"

"No, sir," Teddy said.

"We were hoping you might know the other woman in the photograph?" Nanette asked hopefully.

Mr. Picard looked at the picture again. "Hmmm. Can't say that I do. Hazards of old age, I guess." He handed the picture back to Teddy. "Sorry I can't be more help."

Teddy's shoulders dropped. He held the photo with both hands, his eyes resting heavy on it. Alfie touched his shoulder and said, "Hey, don't worry. We'll figure something out." To Mr. Picard, Alfie said, "Is there anything else you can tell us about Mama Minnie?"

Mr. Picard scratched his chin. "Goodness," he said. "I just always thought her name suited her well. She was such a tiny woman. But she had a laugh that was bigger than this room!"

Teddy and Nanette smiled. Alfie could see they liked hearing this about their grandmother.

"And I sure do miss the pralines she sold over at

Julianne's Candy," Mr. Picard added. "That's what she bought the pecans for. We had a little deal—I'd give her a discount on the pecans, and she'd bring me a few of those pralines. Best in the city!"

"I didn't know she used to sell pralines," Nanette said to Teddy. "Did you?"

Teddy shook his head. "Is Julianne's still around?"

"Of course," Mr. Picard said. "Been around since 1913, and it isn't going anywhere, not if the people of New Orleans have anything to say about it. It's over on St. Philip Street, close to Decatur."

"We have to go there!" Emilia said. "Maybe they know something."

"For sure!" Nanette agreed.

"So what are we waiting for?" Alfie said, eager to follow the next clue in their mystery.

"Thank you for your help, Mr. Picard," Teddy said.

"You're very welcome. Stop by anytime. Minnie's family is always welcome here!"

They headed back out to the street. Alfie was excited. He felt like a real live detective. "That was amazing!" he said. "Even though he doesn't know who the other woman is, he knew lots of stuff about your grandma!"

"Yeah!" Nanette agreed. "I never knew Mama Minnie sold her pralines."

"And maybe if Mr. Picard is still around, Julianne is, too!" Alfie said.

"He said Julianne's Candy has been around since 1913," Emilia said. "I doubt she's still alive."

"Still," Alfie said, refusing to lose hope so early in the hunt. "Someone might know something."

"Let's walk down to the river," Teddy said. "We can cut across to Decatur and get some beignets on the way. You had beignets yet?" he asked Alfie and Emilia.

They both shook their heads.

"I can't believe it! What did you eat during your school trip, because it sure doesn't sound like it was New Orleans food!"

Alfie and Emilia gladly followed their hosts through the city streets. Alfie took note of the street names as they walked. He liked getting familiar with his surroundings. He would have no trouble finding his way through New Orleans alone—all the streets were in a grid pattern.

Soon they were looking out at the Mississippi River. A man in sunglasses and a fedora similar to Nanette's sat in a folding chair and played the saxophone for people walking down by the river. Behind him a riverboat cruised through the water with a wheel turning at the back.

"That's the kind of boat our parents are on," Teddy noted. "Some of them just cruise around the city, and some go all the way up the Mississippi to St. Louis and even Minneapolis."

"It's one of the biggest rivers in the world," Alfie added, thinking about the maps peppering the walls of his room back home.

"Here we are," Teddy said. They were at a small café that looked like it served only one thing besides coffee—

fresh, square powdered doughnuts.

"These are beignets," Nanette told Alfie and Emilia. "They're like doughnuts, but a little different. A New Orleans must-have. Come on, let's get some."

Alfie and Emilia followed Nanette and Teddy into the café, where they ordered four servings. They were given a small paper plate piled with several fried beignets and topped with an avalanche of powdered sugar. They walked back out to the sidewalk and sat at a table outside. Just then, a big brass band led a parade of people down the center of the street. Alfie smiled as he watched the passing crowd dance and sing.

Alfie picked up a warm beignet and bit into a corner. He thought about the zeppole Zia had made that transported them to Naples. Even though both were made with fried dough and sugar, they were totally different. The beignet was much fluffier and not so dense. And the powdered sugar was a different kind of sweet than the mix of cinnamon, sugar, and nutmeg on the zeppole.

"It might just be fried dough," Teddy said. "But I could eat them every day."

"And really, who doesn't love fried dough?" Nanette said.

"With sugar on top!" Alfie added, taking another bite and getting powdered sugar all over his clothes and even on his hat. He didn't know which he liked better—zeppole or beignets. And he hoped he never had to choose!

Chapter 9

A white sign with red lettering hung from the side of a brick building: JULIANNE'S HANDMADE CANDY SINCE 1913.

The kids stepped inside the small store. The white marble countertops were covered in glass and displayed a dizzying array of handmade candy. Alfie enjoyed the cool, air-conditioned space and took in the scene. There was an entire case of truffles with fillings like butterscotch, peanut butter, and banana. And there were just as many different kinds of pralines: chocolate, maple, coconut, Creole, and traditional. Alfie had never had a praline before, and even though he'd just eaten a mountain of powdered sugar, he was eager to try one.

Emilia had already glued herself to the glass in front of the truffles. "Wow," she said.

"Hi there, kids." A woman a little older than their parents came out from the back of the store. Alfie could see through the open doorway that all the candy was made right there. "Looking for something special or just a quick treat?"

"Something special, for sure," Teddy said, carefully pulling out the photograph. "Are you Julianne?"

The woman laughed. "Goodness, no," she said. "I'm Clarice, Julianne's great-granddaughter. Julianne passed away ages ago."

"Wow! Her great-granddaughter!" Emilia exclaimed.

Teddy put the photograph on the counter in front of Clarice. "Well, we were hoping someone could tell us who the woman in this picture is—next to our grandmother, Minnie La Salle?"

"Minnie La Salle? Well, why didn't you say so! And you're her grandkids?" She looked from Teddy and

Nanette to Alfie and Emilia. "I think maybe two are and two aren't," she said, smiling. She picked up the photograph. "Oh, sweet Minnie. We all miss her so much. And here she is with Delphine. I haven't seen Delphine in ages."

"Delphine?" Nanette said.

"Minnie and Delphine used to come in together all the time, especially when they were first learning to cook. They'd drop off a crawfish potpie or jambalaya for my mama to taste, along with the pralines Minnie used to sell us. They said we were their guinea pigs for all the new dishes they were learning!"

Alfie watched Teddy and Nanette's faces light up. Even he enjoyed hearing this new information about Mama Minnie.

"So Mama Minnie and Delphine learned to cook together?" Teddy asked.

"That's right," Clarice said.

"Who taught them?" Nanette asked.

Clarice glanced at the ceiling. "Hmmm. I can't remember her name. She's long since passed, but she was a very interesting woman. Everybody said she used magic in her cooking and that's what made it so great."

Alfie and Emilia exchanged a quick smile. They knew a little something about magic.

"Do you know anything about the book Mama Minnie is holding?" Alfie asked, pointing to the picture.

Clarice put on her glasses and looked again. She shook her head. "I don't think I ever saw Minnie or Delphine with a recipe book. They seemed to have all that knowledge in their heads."

Teddy nodded slowly, looking disappointed.

"Do you know where Delphine is?" Emilia asked. "Teddy and Nanette would love to talk to her about their grandma."

"I haven't seen Delphine in quite a while." Clarice

frowned. "She used to be in the city a lot, doing catering gigs for her longtime clients. She just loved being in the kitchen—maybe even more than Minnie. But as far as I know, she hasn't done any catering in months. Not sure why . . ."

Alfie felt defeated. They were so close to finding answers!

"Oh well," Nanette said, her eyes downcast. "We tried."

"I guess," Teddy mumbled, turning toward the door.

"Seriously, guys? That's it? You're giving up?" Emilia said.

"It's called a dead end," Alfie said. "What else can we do?"

"Keep trying," Emilia said. "Keep thinking." She thought for a moment. "Hey, I know! Ms. Clarice, do you happen to know any of the people Delphine used to do catering for? Maybe they know where she is."

Alfie had to admit, his sister was not only persistent but also smart.

"Well, now, let me think," Clarice said. "It's been so long. I haven't seen Delphine since before your grandma Minnie's service—which was lovely, by the way. The songs you and your family performed in her honor were just breathtaking."

"Thank you," Nanette said.

"But maybe . . . ," Clarice continued. "You know, I do remember Delphine mentioning a party she did once for the Lind family over in the Garden District. I remember because Delphine joked that Mrs. Lind was hopeless in the kitchen before she met Delphine. It might be worth a try, checking in with them."

"Awesome!" Emilia cheered. "I knew it wasn't over!"

"Okay, you were right," Alfie said, thrilled to have another clue to follow. "Do you know where in the Garden District the Linds live, exactly?"

"Can't help you there," Clarice said. "But it shouldn't be too hard to figure out. They're one of the oldest families in the city. Hardly a month goes by without them having a party or charity event at their home. Just ask around, you'll find it."

"Thank you so much, Ms. Clarice," Nanette said.

"Yeah, you've been a lifesaver," Teddy agreed.

"My pleasure," she said. "Anything for Minnie's grandkids. In fact, why don't you all pick something out to take with you—my treat."

Everyone was more than happy to sample the candy despite the beignets, grits, eggs, and sausage they'd already had that day. After all, investigating was hard work!

They all chose something different in order to share bites. Teddy went for the classic praline, while Nanette said there was nothing better than the Creole version with its extra sugar and butter. Alfie chose a Mississippi Mud, which was a large square of dark chocolate with caramel, pecans, and more chocolate. Emilia grabbed a milk-chocolate turtle. Clarice gave her two, "because they're so small," she said.

Everyone thanked Clarice for her help.

"You come back anytime!" she said. "And when you find Delphine, be sure to tell her she better come see me."

The gang walked back out into the strong afternoon sun. The day definitely was getting hotter, but Alfie was eager to keep going. "Let's go find this Lind house!" he said.

"I think we better go home and check in first," Nanette said. "It's getting late, and we have to play tonight, after all."

"Yeah, let's go home and look up the Lind house online. Then we can go grab po'boys for dinner before we head to the club," Teddy said.

"Who are they?" Emilia asked.

"Who?" Teddy said. "You mean *what*."

"You mean to tell us you haven't had a po'boy, either?" Nanette said, her hand on her hip.

Alfie and Emilia looked guiltily at Teddy and Nanette. "Guess not," said Alfie.

"You better call that aunt of yours," Nanette said. "Because you're eating dinner with us tonight."

"Yeah!" Teddy added. "Might as well see if you can stay another night. That way we can go find the Lind house first thing in the morning."

"Sounds good to me," said Alfie. More food and more adventure was just what he was hoping for.

Chapter 10

Alfie, Emilia, Teddy, and Nanette gathered around the La Salles' computer and searched for the Lind home in the Garden District. There were tons of mentions of the Lind family and all the parties and fund-raisers they threw, but no address. Finally, when it started to get late, and Teddy said he was getting hungry, Alfie spotted the name of the street the Linds lived on in an old *Southern Living* magazine article.

"Well, we still don't have the address, but it's something," Teddy said, closing the Internet browser. "We'll just have to go to Chestnut Street tomorrow and ask around."

"Sounds like it's more of a mansion than a house," Alfie added. "That shouldn't be too hard to find!"

Virgil peeked his head around the corner. "You grabbing dinner soon, Teddy? We're starving!"

"Yep!" Teddy jumped up. "We're getting po'boys from Jack's."

"Good choice." Virgil smiled. "Are you two staying for dinner?"

Teddy intercepted. "Yes, and they want to stay the night again, too. We've got more work to do on this photograph."

"I want to hear all about what you found out today when you get back from Jack's," Virgil said. "But in the meantime, Alfie and Emilia need to call their aunt. I want to make sure she's okay with them being gone so long."

"No problem!" Alfie said quickly. "Ready, Teddy?"

"Let's go."

Alfie and Teddy crossed Elysian Fields and walked over to the block past Washington Square Park to Jack's Po'boys. Alfie was still trying to figure out how to dodge Virgil's questions about their aunt. Once inside the tiny sandwich shop, Alfie stared at the menu board. "I have no idea what to order," he told Teddy.

"How 'bout I just order a bunch with fried shrimp and some with fried oysters? Sound good?"

"Perfect!" Alfie said, looking around the shop. There was a pay phone by the restroom, which gave him an idea. "While you order, I'm just going to give my aunt a call." He motioned over to the phone.

"Okay," Teddy said, distracted by placing their order.

Alfie went over to the corner and made sure Teddy wasn't watching. He stood by the phone for a couple of minutes, and then rejoined Teddy at the edge of the counter.

"All set," he said. "She's working late again, so she's happy we're staying."

"Great!" Teddy said.

When they got back to the La Salle house, they spread out the po'boys on the table. Each one was made on a French bread roll with shredded lettuce, tomatoes, pickles, mayonnaise, and Crystal Hot Sauce. Alfie tried one with fried shrimp while Emilia tried the fried oysters.

"I haven't been hungry once since I met you guys," Alfie said, taking a bite of his sandwich. The shrimp were perfectly fried, but not greasy, and the bread was fluffy on the inside and crispy on the outside. The hot sauce wasn't too spicy and added a bit of a vinegary aftertaste. Alfie loved it.

"That's how we like it here," Rex said. "If your stomach starts to grumble, we've done something wrong."

"So tell us how it went at Mr. Picard's today," Jules said.

Teddy told his brothers about going from Mr. Picard's grocery to Julianne's Candy, and the great things Mr.

Picard and Clarice had said about Mama Minnie.

"And then Clarice said that Delphine used to cook for the Linds over in the Garden District," Teddy said, finishing up the story. "So we want to head over there tomorrow and see if we can find out how to get in touch with her."

"I'm impressed," said Jules. "Y'all got a lot of good info today. It's been a long time, but now I think I can remember Mama Minnie cooking with somebody else when we were small. That must have been Delphine. Don't you think, Virg?"

"Huh?" Virgil looked up from his sandwich. Alfie thought he seemed really distracted, like he hadn't actually been listening to any of Teddy's story. He took in all their faces. "Sorry," he said.

"What's wrong?" Nanette asked.

Virgil sighed and pushed the rest of his sandwich away. "I just got a call from Mrs. Ellsworth. The catering company she hired for the masquerade ball had a kitchen fire this afternoon. They can't cater the ball. And Mrs. Ellsworth can't find another caterer on such short notice, so she has to cancel the whole thing."

"What?" Jules cried. "They can't cancel it! We need that gig."

"What's going on?" Alfie asked.

"Every year at the end of Jazz Fest the Ellsworths have a big masquerade ball. Mama Minnie used to cater it, and we've always played music at the ball. They found a new caterer after Mama Minnie died, but kept us on as the musicians," Teddy explained.

"We were counting on that money to pay Charlie what we owe him," Virgil added. "Now we're definitely going to be short."

Everybody sat in silence for a while, no longer hungry.

Finally Emilia spoke up. "Now we *have* to find the Lind house and talk to Delphine!"

"Why?" Jules asked.

"What if there really is a recipe book?" Emilia said.

"What good is that going to do us now?" Virgil asked. "And I really doubt that it would be Minnie's book, anyway. She was always so adamant about never writing down any recipes."

"I still think it's worth a shot," Emilia said. "Maybe there's no recipe book. But maybe there is, and that's pretty big, don't you think? To have all your grandmother's recipes when you thought you had none? That's huge."

"She's right," said Rex. "It's Mama Minnie's legacy, which means it's our legacy, too."

"Maybe Gus and the other cooks could learn her recipes in time for next year's masquerade ball. Then you could do the music *and* the food!" Alfie said. "Not to mention, you could use her recipes at La Salle Royale to bring customers back!"

"And even if there's no book, maybe Delphine can tell us stories about her," Nanette said.

"Or teach us to cook," Rex added.

"Okay." Virgil held up his hands in surrender. "Go to the Lind house tomorrow and see what you can find. Now we better focus on tonight. It's time to get ready to go."

Everybody scrambled up from the table to get dressed for La Salle Royale. Virgil turned around in the doorway. "Oh, Alfie and Emilia, let's call your aunt real quick."

Alfie's face got warm. "I already did. When Teddy and I went out to get the po'boys. Right, Teddy?"

"Huh?" Teddy said. "Oh, yeah, there was a pay phone at Jack's."

Virgil sighed. "I'd feel a lot better if I actually talked to your aunt."

"She was on her way to work." Alfie shrugged. "She wanted me to thank you for letting us stay again. She said she really appreciates it and knows we're in good hands."

"All right," Virgil conceded. "But if you're planning on staying past tomorrow, I'm gonna need to talk to her myself."

Alfie nodded, remembering their time in Paris. There was only so long you could keep the adults from asking too many questions.

Chapter 11

The next morning, the four detectives set out to find the Lind mansion in the Garden District. They boarded the St. Charles Avenue streetcar and sat on glossy wooden seats beneath exposed lightbulbs on the ceiling. The trees along the streetcar line were dotted with Mardi Gras beads. The green, pink, and purple beads looked like they'd been hanging there for months or even years—the colors were faded by the sun. The city was lively enough during Jazz Fest—Alfie couldn't imagine what it must be like during Mardi Gras!

They hopped off at Jackson Avenue and walked a few blocks toward Chestnut Street. Alfie picked up two sticks from the ground and started tapping them along the fences as they walked.

"Hey, that sounds like a jazz rhythm!" Teddy said.

Alfie beamed. "Really? I just started learning to play the drums back home. I'd love to learn some jazz songs."

"Too bad Dad's gone this weekend," Nanette said. "He's a great teacher."

Just then, a woman rushed past them on the sidewalk, eyes on her phone. Nanette stopped and said, "Excuse me. Do you know where the Lind house is?"

"Sorry, I don't," she responded quickly and kept walking.

When they reached Chestnut, Alfie spotted a man across the street walking his dog. "Sir?" he called out. The dog wagged his tail as Alfie approached. "Do you happen to know the Lind house?"

"Sure!" the man said cheerfully. "It's a big white house on the corner of Third, just a few blocks up. Can't miss it."

The man's dog licked Alfie's hand. He bent down to give the dog a quick scratch under the chin. Then the dog grabbed one of Alfie's sticks and started playing tug-of-war. Alfie laughed as the dog growled playfully. "Okay, you win!" Alfie finally said, letting go of the stick. "Thanks for your help," he told the man.

Alfie dropped the other stick and rejoined the detective team with a proud look on his face. "It's just a couple of blocks this way, on Third."

"Good work!" said Teddy.

They passed First and Second Streets, quickly reaching the corner of Third. A huge two-story, white columned house sat on a rich green lawn with a big weeping willow shading part of the upstairs balcony. There was a wrought iron fence, made to look like a row of cornstalks, ringing the property. A van was parked in front of the house, and a woman was carrying some folding chairs from the house to the van.

"This is definitely a mansion," Alfie said, taking in the house. "It has to be the one."

They stopped next to the van, and Teddy spoke to the

woman. "Excuse me, ma'am? Is this the Lind house?"

"Yes it is," she said as she pushed the chairs into the van.

"Great. Thanks!"

Emilia passed through the gate and walked up the sidewalk like she was going home.

"I like your sister," Nanette told Alfie. "She doesn't hesitate when she sets her mind on something."

Alfie laughed. Emilia was definitely getting much bolder thanks to all their new adventures.

Emilia stepped up onto the large wooden porch and rang the doorbell. The others stood behind her and waited. Soon the heavy black door swung open, and a woman in a floral-print dress peered out at them. "Can I help you?" she asked.

"Hello," Emilia said. "We're looking

for Mrs. Lind. We wanted to ask her a question about a photograph."

"Please come in," the woman said.

The kids shuffled into the foyer. "Please wait here and I'll tell Mrs. Lind," the woman said.

Alfie couldn't believe how grand and beautiful the house was. It had marble floors and looked even more like a movie set than the La Salles' house did.

A minute later, the woman returned, followed by another, older woman with perfectly styled white hair.

"Hello, kids," she said. "I'm Margaret Lind. What can I do for you?"

"I'm Emilia and these are my friends, Teddy and Nanette La Salle. You might know them from the club their family has in the French Quarter—La Salle Royale? Oh, and this is my little brother, Alfredo."

Alfie grimaced at the use of his full name.

"Nice to meet you all," Mrs. Lind said, seeming a bit confused.

Teddy stepped forward with the photograph in his hand. "We were hoping you could help us. This is our grandmother, Mama Minnie. And Clarice over at Julianne's Candy said you might know the other woman in the picture, Delphine?"

"Goodness," Mrs. Lind said. "Sounds like you are on quite a mission this afternoon."

"Yes, ma'am," Nanette said. "Do you know Delphine?"

"Certainly, I do." Mrs. Lind smiled, her light blue eyes shining bright. "As a matter of fact, I was just heating up some lunch—a recipe that Delphine taught me. Why don't you join me in the kitchen?"

They followed Mrs. Lind across the marble floor and into the kitchen.

"Delphine was like family to us. Still is. We just don't see her much anymore. Not since her husband passed away. Poor dear."

"When did he pass away?" Nanette asked quietly.

"About six months ago," Mrs. Lind said, turning from

the stove. "They were inseparable, Simon and Delphine.
In fact, I bet he's the one who took that picture."

"Is she okay?" Emilia asked. "Delphine?"

Mrs. Lind looked back into the steaming pot. "I wish
I knew. We've only seen her once since Simon's funeral.
I told her to come by the house anytime and we'd cook
together. She used to love showing me new Creole or
Cajun dishes. We had so much fun in the kitchen—she

taught me everything I know. I couldn't make scrambled eggs before I met Delphine!"

The woman who'd been loading the van appeared in the kitchen doorway. "That's everything, Mrs. Lind."

"Thank you so much, Caroline," Mrs. Lind said warmly. "It was a great little party."

"You're welcome," Caroline said. "See you soon."

Mrs. Lind faced the kids. "Caroline helped me throw a small party for my husband's birthday yesterday. It's funny you're here today because I made étouffée. It was the first real dish Delphine taught me to cook. And it's my husband's favorite, so I make it every year for his birthday." She smiled and stirred the pot. "And it's almost better the second day. I've got plenty of leftovers. Would you all like to try some?"

"We'd love to," Nanette said. "Thank you."

"My brother and I are just visiting," Emilia said. "So we don't know much about New Orleans food. What exactly is *ay-too-fey*?" She said the word carefully like she was afraid of mispronouncing it.

"Étouffée is a little bit like gumbo, but with a thicker sauce, and it's usually made with only one type of seafood. This is a crawfish étouffée," Mrs. Lind said, putting a small scoop of white rice in the bottom of five bowls and then adding a bit of the stewlike dish on top. She passed the dishes to everyone.

"Étouffée," Emilia said again, working out the pronunciation. "It sounds French."

"That's right," Mrs. Lind said. "It is—the word translates to *smothered*. Basically we're just smothering this crawfish in the tomato-base sauce."

Alfie blew lightly on his steaming bowl. When he took a bite, he could immediately tell the difference between this and the gumbo he and Emilia had helped Zia make. In addition to the crawfish, the étouffée had a creamy, gravy-like sauce. The gumbo was more like a soup. But they both tasted amazing!

"I guess our next stop is Delphine's house then!" Alfie said to the others between bites. He wondered which neighborhood she lived in. All the neighborhoods in New Orleans seemed so different from one another.

"Would you mind giving us her address?" Emilia asked Mrs. Lind.

"I'm afraid I can't help you there," Mrs. Lind said. "It sounds crazy, but I don't know where she lives! Well, I know where—out on the bayou just outside town. But I've never been to her house and never thought to ask for her address. She always came to us."

Alfie couldn't believe it. They were so close! He knew they all had the sense that Delphine held some answers about Mama Minnie—recipes or not. They knew now that Delphine learned to cook with Minnie and probably knew her cooking best. They wanted to meet her and hear her stories about Mama Minnie. But if the only address Mrs. Lind had for her was "out on the bayou," then they were at a dead end.

"Can you think of anyone else who might know where

she lives?" Emilia asked, not wanting to give up.

Mrs. Lind shook her head. "Like I said, Delphine always came to us. She was here in town so often it was easy to forget she drove in each day. Now I wish I'd thought to ask. I'd love to go visit her. I'm sorry I'm not more helpful."

"You've been *so* helpful!" Nanette said.

"Really," said Teddy. "Thank you."

"And thanks for the delicious food!" Alfie added. Everybody grinned and nodded as they finished their bowls.

Afterward, Mrs. Lind walked them to the front door. "I knew I missed Delphine, but I didn't realize how much until today. If you see her, please tell her to stop by."

"We will," Nanette said.

They waved good-bye as they walked back down the brick path to the front gate. Their steps were a lot slower and heavier this time. Alfie didn't know what they would do next. The trail had gone cold.

Chapter 12

"We were so close," Teddy said as they walked down Chestnut Street. "There has to be something we can do!"

Nanette draped her arm around Teddy's shoulder. "We'll keep looking. Maybe if we start asking around at the club someone will eventually know Delphine and can tell us where she lives."

Alfie and Emilia exchanged a quick look. They were frustrated that the mystery hadn't been solved. And Alfie was beginning to wonder how long it might take. They'd enjoyed their time in New Orleans, but they didn't want to stay *too* long.

"I'm kind of thirsty," Teddy said. "Y'all want to get

something to drink before heading back?"

"A cold drink sounds good," Alfie said.

They walked over to Magazine Street and stopped at a little café that had metal tables lined up on the sidewalk. Alfie and Nanette got lemonade, and Teddy and Emilia got sweet tea. They sat outside and watched people wander in and out of the nearby stores selling art, jewelry, antiques, and clothing. Alfie watched two moms with fussy babies in strollers stop to chat on the sidewalk. This area reminded him a little bit of Main Street back home.

Suddenly, a woman stopped beside their table.

"Weren't you just at Mrs. Lind's house? Talking about Delphine?" the woman asked, shading her eyes from the sun.

"Yes," Alfie said. It was Caroline—the woman with the van. Alfie hadn't realized she'd heard them talking. Now her van was parked in front of the café, and a man was bringing the tables and chairs into a party-supply store next door.

"Why y'all looking for Delphine, anyway?" Caroline
asked. Alfie thought she seemed a little suspicious of them.

Teddy pulled the photograph from his pocket and
handed it to her. "That's Delphine along with our
grandmother Minnie. Our grandmother passed away last
year, and we just wanted to talk to Delphine about her."

Caroline took the photo. "You must be the La Salle kids, then."

"Yes," Nanette said, looking hopeful. "I'm Nanette, and this is Teddy."

"I haven't been down to La Salle Royale in ages. Used to have the best red beans and rice in town."

Teddy and Nanette nodded and focused on their empty glasses. "We know."

Caroline glanced up and down the street, like she didn't want to get in trouble. "Well, I know where Delphine lives."

"You do!?" the four kids cried together.

Caroline held up her hands. "I do. But she doesn't much like visitors at all these days."

"Please," Alfie said. "They just want to hear a little more about their grandmother."

Caroline sighed. "Oh, all right," she said. "Got a pen?"

Teddy ran into the café and asked for a pen and a piece of paper. Caroline scribbled down some notes. "There's no real address," she told them. "But it's about two miles off the byway, past a little seafood shack called Sargent Sassafras. Delphine's place is called Sleeping Waters."

She handed the paper and pen to Teddy. "Be careful going up to the door. Like I said, she doesn't like unexpected visitors."

Alfie thought that sounded a little sketchy. "Do you have her number so we can call first?"

Caroline shook her head. "She never gives it out. That's how much she doesn't like to be bothered."

Alfie nodded and turned to Emilia, Teddy, and Nanette. They all had very determined looks on their faces. They'd come this far. They couldn't turn back now.

They thanked Caroline, and she walked toward her shop. "Good luck!" she called over her shoulder.

Chapter 13

"We can't go to the bayou," Teddy said as they boarded the St. Charles Avenue streetcar. "At least, not on our own. We'll need a car to get outside the city, so that means Virgil will have to drive us."

"I doubt he'll agree to it," Nanette said, sliding down in her seat.

"Why not?" Emilia asked.

"He's so stressed about the club," Nanette said. "Driving out to the bayou is the last thing he's going to want to do this afternoon."

"It doesn't hurt to ask," Emilia said.

Once they got back to the house, they gathered the

brothers and told them what they'd learned.

"I can't believe it!" Rex said. "Y'all really did it."

"Not yet," Nanette said. "But we're close."

They really were—Alfie almost couldn't believe it,
either. They'd gone from finding a photograph they
didn't know existed to discovering the woman Mama

Minnie learned to cook with to now finding out where that woman lived. Even if the address was just "Sleeping Waters, Bayou, Louisiana," they were onto something.

"Now we just need you to drive us out to the bayou so we can visit her," Teddy said to Virgil, as if he was just asking him to run to the corner store for a bag of chips.

Virgil rubbed his eyes and looked tired. "Y'all have done a real good job. I can't believe how much you've learned. But going out to the bayou without an address? That just sounds crazy."

"Come on, Virg, you know how those homes are out there," Jules said. "It's normal for them to have names instead of numbers."

"I know," he said. "But how do you think this woman is going to feel about a bunch of kids showing up on her porch asking questions? At the very least, it's rude."

"We'll call first!" Jules said, getting excited.

"Well, that's the thing," Nanette said. "We don't have her phone number."

Virgil raised his hands as if his point had been made.

An air of defeat hung over the room. Alfie's mind raced to come up with a solution.

"Look," Virgil said. "I know you want to meet Delphine. But guys—she's not Mama Minnie. She can't replace her."

"We know," Nanette muttered.

Emilia jumped to her feet. "But what if Delphine *could* replace Mama Minnie—as the caterer for the masquerade ball!"

Teddy jumped up, too. "Yeah! Then we could still play the gig!"

"We may not come back from the bayou with Mama Minnie's recipes, but we might be able to come back with a chef for the party!" Nanette added.

Everyone watched Virgil carefully.

"Worth a shot," Rex said, smiling.

Finally, Virgil sighed and stood up, too. "Okay," he said. "Let's go."

Chapter 14

They rode out of town in Mama Minnie's old boat of a car across the expansive Crescent City Connection and over the Mississippi River with their windows down, letting the warm wind race across their faces. Virgil and Teddy sat in the front, with Alfie, Emilia, and Nanette in the back. Jules and Rex had stayed behind, begrudgingly. Virgil didn't like the idea of so many people showing up unannounced on Delphine's porch. He thought they were pushing the boundaries of hospitality as it was—even for Louisiana.

Before long they were out of the city and crossing another bridge, this time into the water-soaked lands of the Louisiana bayou.

Alfie watched as they passed neighborhoods
that looked similar to the ones back home. Those
neighborhoods gave way to sparser ones surrounded
by ropes of water. They passed homes built on stilts
to protect from storm surges and rising rivers—the
first floor was up where the second or even third floor
might be, with cars parked under the house. Many of
the homes had names—Basin Bliss, Under the Cajun
Moon, Evangeline's *A Bon Coeur*. To Alfie it seemed as
foreign and exciting as anything else he'd seen on their
adventures.

"Keep your eyes open," Virgil said, turning slowly onto a narrow road just beyond the seafood shack Caroline had told them about. They were close.

Thick trees hung over the road blocking out the sun. Alfie kept his eyes on the woods, searching for any signs of Delphine's home. Suddenly, he spotted something.

"Look!" he shouted, pointing to a small moss-covered wooden sign with faded black letters that said SLEEPING WATERS. Virgil turned down the dirt-and-gravel driveway, the car bumping and dipping into puddles as they went.

They stopped when they came to a creek blocking the way to the house, which was tucked back behind a curtain of weeping willows and live oak trees. Virgil parked the car and shut off the engine. They all climbed out.

Virgil led the way across the footbridge that arched over the creek. "Careful," he said, stepping over missing boards.

The last thing Alfie wanted was to slip through the bridge. Weren't there alligators in the bayou?

They stepped up onto the small porch next to two old rocking chairs. Colored glass bottles and wind chimes made of what looked like bone hung above them, softly tinkling in the breeze. Alfie didn't want to think about what kind of bone the chimes might be. He glanced at Emilia, who seemed as nervous as he was.

"Let me do the talking," Virgil said as he knocked on the front door. The only noises they heard as they waited were the sounds of crickets, frogs, and other strange creatures Alfie preferred not to think about.

Finally, the door creaked open. A set of dark eyes peered back at them. Alfie's heart thumped in his chest. He reached out for Emilia's hand. Maybe this hadn't been such a good idea after all.

Virgil cleared his throat. "Hello—Miss Delphine?"

"Who wants to know?" a sharp voice said. "Because whatever you're selling, I'm not buying."

"We're not selling anything," Virgil said. "We're looking for Delphine—we were told she might know our grandmother." Teddy held up the photo they'd carried with them all over New Orleans.

"You're Minnie La Salle's grandkids, aren't you?" she said before she even looked at the photograph.

"Yes, ma'am," Virgil said.

Delphine pushed open the screen door. "Well, then you're just in time," she said. "Come on in and eat with me."

Alfie let out a sigh of relief and followed the others into the house. There weren't many lights on inside, and Alfie had to let his eyes adjust. His nose, however, got it right away. Something was cooking.

She led them into a small kitchen—so different from Mrs. Lind's grand space from earlier that day. "Now let's see," she said. "You must be Virgil, and Nanette, and Teddy." She pointed at the three La Salle children. They all nodded and smiled. "I remember when you were about this high, Virgil." Delphine held her hand a few feet above the floor. "You were always tugging on the hem of Minnie's dress asking for a snack."

Teddy and Nanette laughed. Virgil looked embarrassed.

"And what about you two?" Delphine said to Alfie and Emilia.

"They're our friends," Teddy told her. "Alfie and Emilia. They're visiting their aunt in New Orleans."

"Well, welcome to Sleeping Waters. Have a seat." Delphine motioned to the small wooden table in the middle of the room. She went to the stove and dropped battered pieces of meat into a cast-iron frying pan. "I remember the first time Minnie and I learned to cook with alligator tail," she began. "You can fry it, grill

it, put it in gumbo, jambalaya, étouffée—really anything you're putting meat in. We made all kinds of crazy dishes just trying to get our rhythm." Delphine laughed at the memory. After a few more minutes, she removed the fried meat from the pan and set it on a plate. She brought the plate over to the center of the table and placed a small dish of sauce next to it. "Go ahead, don't be shy."

They each picked up a piece of meat and dipped it into the sauce. The meat was juicy with a slightly oily taste, and the thick sauce was lemony with a spicy kick that Alfie immediately liked.

"Yep," Delphine said, pulling up a chair to the table. "You can do a lot of things with alligator tail." She picked up a piece of meat and popped it into her mouth. Which got Alfie thinking . . .

"Excuse me, Miss Delphine?" he said. "What kind of meat is this?"

"Alligator tail, of course," she said. Alfie looked quickly at Emilia. Before Zia Donatella had come to stay with them, they might have thought it was weird or gross to eat this. Now Alfie loved to be adventurous and try new foods. And this was *way* better than the "thousand-year-old egg" he'd tried in Hong Kong!

"Minnie and I hadn't seen as much of each other in recent years," Delphine said. "She was busy with you grandkids and cooking at the club, and my husband and I were busy with our catering work. But Minnie's service was so lovely," she continued. "A real tribute to her life. I had planned to come by and bring food to your family, but then my husband got sick . . ."

"Simon, right?" Nanette said carefully. "We're so sorry."

"Yes," Delphine said. "My Simon. Life just didn't have the same joy once he and Minnie were gone. I haven't been cooking much since then. They were the two people I loved cooking with the most."

"Everyone is still talking about your cooking," Teddy said. "We were at Mrs. Lind's house this morning—she made étouffée for her husband's birthday."

Delphine smiled. "She makes it for him every year. When I met her, she couldn't cook to save her life!"

The kids laughed. "She told us," Emilia said. "She also told us she misses you. She wants you to come and visit her soon."

"Everyone in town misses you," Teddy said.

"And your cooking," Alfie added.

"I have to say," Delphine said, looking at the now-empty plate on the table. "It feels good to cook for other people again. That's the beauty of cooking—it's not just nourishment for your body, it's nourishment for your soul."

"That's how it always felt with Mama Minnie," Teddy said. "Like she wasn't just cooking for us, she was giving us something special."

"I think that's how everyone felt coming into La Salle Royale, too," Virgil added.

"Minnie's cooking was special, all right," Delphine said. "I always said it's not something you can get by following a recipe. Funny I say that, though, since I'm the one who told Minnie we should write down our recipes."

"I'm sorry, what did you say?" Virgil asked. Alfie held his breath.

"I told Minnie we should write down our recipes," Delphine repeated. "But do you think she listened to me? No sir. She was stubborn, your grandmother."

The kids sighed. "We wish she had," Virgil said. "We were really hoping to find something of hers."

"Something like a recipe book?" Delphine asked. "Minnie never wanted to record the things she made." She pushed back from the table and walked into another room. The others looked questioningly at each other. When she came back, she surprised them all by saying, "But I did."

In her hands was a book that looked a lot like the one in the picture with which they'd all become so familiar. Alfie couldn't believe it. And based on everybody else's wide eyes, they couldn't, either.

"When we were still learning, I wrote everything

down," Delphine said. "Minnie told me I was crazy, that she knew all the recipes by heart. But the more I recorded what we knew, the more she understood that it wasn't

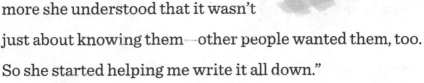

just about knowing them—other people wanted them, too. So she started helping me write it all down."

Teddy slowly pulled the book toward him and picked it up as if it were a precious treasure. Alfie supposed that it was. "I can't believe it," he said, opening the pages.

"I've had this book for years," Delphine said.

Nanette looked at the pages with Teddy. "It's amazing."

"I'm so glad y'all came out to see me today. Now this book can go home with you. I hope you'll put it to use," said Delphine.

"Oh, we will!" Teddy said. "Thank you."

"Miss Delphine," Virgil began. "Would you consider cooking at La Salle Royale tonight? Our patrons would love it. They miss Minnie's cooking something fierce. And maybe you would enjoy cooking for people again, too."

"Oh, I don't know," Delphine said.

"I don't want to push you," Virgil said. "But you could try it just for one night. And if you don't like it, then you stop."

"It's been so long," Delphine said. "But you're right. You've reminded me today that nothing makes me feel better than cooking for others."

Everyone was quiet while Delphine thought it over. Finally, she agreed. "Okay, I'll do it," she said. "I'll do it for Minnie. She loved that club and you kids so much, and I know how hard y'all work playing your instruments."

"Thank you so much!" Teddy said, hardly able to contain his excitement.

Even Alfie felt like jumping up and down. "Well, what are we waiting for?" he said. "Let's get to the club!"

Chapter 15

On the way back into New Orleans, Alfie, Emilia, and Nanette sat in the backseat going through the pages of Delphine and Mama Minnie's recipe book. Teddy leaned over the seat, looking on.

"Mama Minnie's handwriting is so pretty," Emilia said.

She was right—each word was like a picture, carefully drawn onto the thick pages.

Nanette ran her finger over the words. "I love seeing her writing again."

Delphine had agreed to meet them at the club later that evening.

"What if she changes her mind?" Teddy asked Virgil.

"Then that's her decision," Virgil said. "We can't push her."

When they got back to town, Virgil parked the car, and the others ran inside to tell Rex and Jules the good news.

"I can't believe you little shrimps did all this!" Rex was grinning ear to ear as he paged through the recipe book. "Way to go!"

"You think her cooking will help the club?" Jules asked Virgil.

"We'll just have to see," Virgil said. "But I'm taking a cue from Teddy, Nanette, Alfie, and Emilia here. They've been working hard to find out more about Mama Minnie and her cooking. And they've reminded me just how important the club is. We need to do whatever it takes to save it."

The La Salle family and Alfie and Emilia walked to the club with a spring in their steps that night. When they got there, the band started to warm up while Alfie and Emilia followed Rex into the kitchen to make sure everything was ready.

When Delphine arrived, everybody rushed out of the kitchen to greet her. The kids, the cooks, the dishwashers, and the whole staff cheered and whistled and hollered. And Delphine didn't seem nervous at all. She looked focused and confident—ready to make some of the most authentic New Orleans food in the city.

In the kitchen, Delphine laid out her menu for the evening: crawfish potpie, gumbo, dirty rice, fried chicken, hush puppies, and mac and cheese, with banana bread pudding for dessert. Everybody got to work right away, and in no time, Delphine and the rest of the kitchen crew had fallen into a steady rhythm of prepping, sautéing, stirring, and cooking. Emilia worked on chopping vegetables while Alfie was in charge of putting a garnish on each plate. In between tossing pinches of parsley on each dish, he drummed his fingers against the counter to the beat of the music just outside the swinging door.

Rex stayed close to Delphine while she showed him all the tricks and secrets that made hers and Minnie's cooking so special. "You're a natural," Delphine told him. "You'll be making up your own family recipes to pass down in no time!"

Alfie could see how proud Rex was. He'd found his special talent in the La Salle family, and he was perfectly at home.

The band took a break, and Jules, Teddy, and Nanette raced into the kitchen to try some of Delphine's cooking.

"Delphine, this is amazing!" Jules said, tasting the dirty rice Delphine had just made. "And the customers can already taste the difference, too. Mr. Jackson said he hasn't had gumbo so hearty and flavorful since Mama Minnie was here. When I told him we had a special chef cooking tonight, he said he was calling all his friends and demanding they get down here right now for a bowl of that gumbo!"

"We have plenty for everyone," Delphine said. "I've got Emilia here slicing more andouille sausage as we speak."

Alfie watched Emilia as she concentrated on cutting the sausage into coin-size pieces just like Zia had taught her.

Just then, Virgil rushed into the kitchen, too. "Mr. and Mrs. Ellsworth are here! They said they heard about the fantastic menu tonight and they had to try it for themselves. And the crowd keeps getting bigger and bigger. People who can't get a table tonight are filling up the reservations book weeks in advance. It's amazing!"

"Just goes to show," Alfie said. "La Salle Royale had all the right ingredients for a great club—you just needed the perfect recipe to bring everything together."

"That's right!" Delphine said as she loaded up plates for Virgil to take to Mr. and Mrs. Ellsworth.

The band went back out to play their second set, and the rest of the evening flew by. Alfie heard Virgil thank the crowd for coming and a few minutes later he and the rest of the band burst through the door. "We did it!" Virgil shouted, dancing over to Delphine to kiss her on the cheek. "*You* did it. The Ellsworths loved everything they tasted. Not only do they want us to cater the masquerade ball and play the music, they want to host the party right here at La Salle Royale! Delphine, we owe you everything!"

"We all worked together," Delphine said, a smile spreading across her face.

"So what do you say? Are you up for another night of cooking?" Virgil asked. "Please say yes. I know it's short notice, but I'd love for you to be in charge of the party tomorrow night."

They waited for Delphine's response. Finally she spoke. "I'll help out tomorrow night."

Everybody cheered and clapped. Delphine held up her hand to quiet them. "But I'm an old woman. I can't keep up this pace every night, you know."

"Well, it's a good thing you've got an apprentice then," Rex said.

Delphine beamed. "Yes it is. And I'll teach you everything I know. It's clear you belong in this kitchen, Rex La Salle."

Rex swooped in and kissed Delphine on the other cheek. She laughed and swatted him with a towel. "Now get back to work! We've got a lot to do if we're going to throw this party tomorrow night."

Alfie carried some plates over to the dishwasher and then stole a glance back at Delphine. The look on her face said it all—this was where she belonged, too.

Chapter 16

Alfie put on his mask and looked in the mirror next to the bed in the room he and Emilia had shared during their New Orleans adventure. Teddy and Nanette had given them new outfits and masks to wear for the masquerade ball.

"How do I look?" he asked.

"Mysterious!" Emilia laughed, trying on her own mask.

There was a knock on the door, and Virgil peeked his head in. "With all the excitement last night, I forgot to call your aunt," he said. "I really need to speak to her."

"It's okay," Alfie said. "We were going to tell you that we're actually heading back to her house after the party tonight. We're going home in the morning."

Teddy and Nanette appeared in the doorway behind Virgil.

"Ah, do you have to?" Nanette said.

"We're going to miss you," Teddy said. "Promise you'll keep in touch?"

Alfie and Emilia exchanged a look. "We're going to miss you, too," Emilia said.

"Well, tell your aunt she's welcome at La Salle Royale anytime," Virgil said. "We'd love to meet her."

"We will." Alfie smiled. He knew Zia Donatella would love the jazz club.

Virgil closed the door, leaving Alfie and Emilia alone.

"Do you think we really are going home tonight?" Emilia asked Alfie.

Alfie shrugged. "It seems like it, right? We helped find the recipe book, and everything's going so well at the club now. It feels like the right time. And besides, we can't keep dodging Virgil."

"You're right," Emilia said.

"Now we just have to find the food that can transport us back home!" Alfie said.

"We will," Emilia said with the same confidence she'd had when they were searching for Delphine and the recipes.

Alfie and Emilia headed downstairs to join Jules, Virgil, Teddy, and Nanette, and walk over to the club. Rex was already there helping Delphine with all the preparations.

When they walked inside, they saw the club had been transformed. Royal Mardi Gras colors of purple, green, and gold filled the space, which was illuminated by hundreds of tiny candles. Waiters in black uniforms and black masks bustled around making sure everything was ready. Fluttering among the last-minute chaos was one woman in an elaborate emerald gown with gold trim. Her face lit up when she saw the La Salle family, and she came rushing over.

"You're a genius!" Mrs. Ellsworth cried to Virgil. "How

you got the famous Delphine to come back to town and cook, I'll never know."

"It's a family secret." Virgil laughed.

Alfie smiled. It was true, Delphine was like family to them now.

Alfie and Emilia agreed to help in the kitchen again this evening, but Virgil made it clear that he wanted them to have a good time, too. "Help out as long as you're having fun," he told them. "But go out and enjoy the music, and please—eat the food! I want your last night to be the best yet."

"Thank you for everything, Virgil. We've had a great time!" Alfie said as he and Emilia headed back to the kitchen.

They pushed open the door and took in the frantic, excited scene. It reminded Alfie of the energy of the Parisian cooking-school kitchen right before the big contest, with people bustling all around. And in the center of this kitchen stood Delphine, looking incredibly calm.

"Welcome back!" she said. "You two ready for the big night?"

"We're ready," Emilia replied, tying on an apron. Alfie did the same and took his place at the prep station.

Rex walked up holding a stack of serving trays. He looked just as comfortable as Delphine. "Hey, guys!" he said, a huge bright smile on his face. "I'll bring the food to you and you put it on the trays for the waiters to take out, got it?"

Instead of making dinners like the club normally did, they made trays of little bite-size food. Rex and Delphine had made oysters Bienville, spicy Gulf shrimp, fried asparagus, bacon-wrapped crawfish bites, and of course, fried alligator tail. For dessert they planned to serve beignets, bananas Foster, and Doberge cake. The cake was a very special recipe that Minnie and Delphine had perfected together. With all that amazing food, Alfie had no doubt it would be the best party of the year.

The guests started to arrive, and the party was

underway. "Just look at them!" Emilia said, peeking into the club to see what everyone was wearing. "They're like peacocks!" She was right. The guests were dressed beautifully in tuxedos and fancy gowns. But the best part was the masks—with elaborate sequin details and colorful feathers sprouting out the tops.

"Go on out there," Delphine said when she saw them peeking out the kitchen door.

Alfie and Emilia put on their masks and stepped out into the full energy of the party. The band sounded as beautiful and raucous as the partygoers themselves. A waiter stopped in front of them and offered them a piece of fried asparagus with mustard sauce.

"I can't believe how good this is," Emilia said.

"There's definitely something magical about Delphine's cooking," Alfie agreed. "She kind of reminds me of Zia—don't you think?"

"Totally," said Emilia, taking another bite.

They weaved through the party guests, trying bits

of food from each tray that passed and listening to everybody rave about it. One man said, "I can't wait to get home and write my review. I can see the headline now— 'La Salle Royale Is Back and Better than Ever'!"

They passed Mr. Picard and Clarice from Julianne's Candy laughing and enjoying the food. Then they saw Caroline and Mrs. Lind sneaking into the kitchen to stay hello to Delphine. Alfie was glad they had all come to the party. He felt like it was as much a celebration of Delphine and Mama Minnie as anything else.

During a band break, they spotted Virgil in the corner talking to Charlie. They inched closer to hear what they were saying. Charlie held a plate piled high with food.

"So with the money from tonight's gig and the list of reservations we've got for the coming weeks, we'll have no problem getting you the rent we owe," Virgil was saying.

"That's terrific, Virgil, really," Charlie said between bites of alligator tail. "I'm so thrilled!" The two men shook hands, and then Virgil walked toward Alfie and Emilia.

Alfie thought he seemed more relieved and happy than he had the whole time they'd been there.

Just then Jules hurried over as well. "Ready to start the next set?" he asked Virgil.

"Yep. I was just coming to see if Alfie wanted to join us for a couple of songs on the drums."

"Me?" Alfie wasn't sure he'd heard Virgil right.

"Yes, you!" Virgil laughed. "Teddy told me you were learning. What do you say?"

Alfie's cheeks were warm. "Uh, I don't know. I mean,

I'm really just *starting* to learn . . ."

Emilia nudged his arm. "You can do it! I've seen you drumming with forks, sticks, spoons, anything you can find lately!"

"Come on, little man." Jules put his arm around Alfie's shoulder and led him toward the stage. "Sam will show you an easy rhythm you can hold."

Alfie's heart beat fast in his chest as he sat on Sam's drum stool. Sam had shown him the beat and let him practice a few times, giving him some pointers. Virgil had just switched off the recorded music they put on during the break and stood in front of the microphone. Alfie strained to see out into the crowd—the hot lights were very bright. He could see Emilia standing front and center, waving frantically. That made him feel better.

"Thanks again for coming out tonight, everyone. And thanks to Mr. and Mrs. Ellsworth for the wonderful party!" Virgil said. The audience clapped and cheered.

"Please continue to enjoy the food made by La Salle

Royale's new chef, the one and only Delphine! We've got a bunch more music to play for y'all, so I hope you're ready to start dancing. Oh, and one last thing before we get going, we also have a special guest drummer up here to do a couple of songs with us, so please give a warm welcome to our friend Alfredo Bertolizzi!"

Alfie smiled and waved his drumsticks as the crowd clapped and whistled. He liked hearing his full name amplified across the club. Maybe he would use Alfredo as his musician name. Virgil counted out "one, two, three, four," and the band began to play. Alfie's nervousness melted away as he drummed the beat and started getting into the music.

He played three songs and then Sam appeared to take his place. "You did great!" Sam told him. Alfie walked across the stage, shaking hands with the La Salle kids as he went. He'd never felt happier, or more proud of himself.

When he hopped off the edge of the stage, Emilia threw her arms around him in a big hug, and he actually let her. "You were amazing!" she cried.

They made their way over to the kitchen and pushed the door open. Rex and Delphine grinned at Alfie.

"Way to go!" Rex shouted. "That was awesome!"

"You two get on over here and grab a piece of this Doberge cake before it all disappears," Delphine said. She handed them each a big slice of cake covered in glossy chocolate frosting. The yellow cake had at least eight chocolate layers in between, if Alfie had counted correctly.

"I made it as a special thank-you to y'all for helping me remember how much I love filling people's stomachs and souls with my cooking."

"Thank you, Delphine," Emilia and Alfie said before digging into their cake. They wandered back out to the club to hear the band play.

"This is like the best birthday cake times a hundred," Alfie said, taking another bite of the rich-but-fluffy goodness.

"Remember that chocolate cake Dad tried to make as a surprise for my tenth birthday?" Emilia said.

Alfie laughed. "I still can't believe the fire department didn't show up—there was so much smoke in the kitchen!"

"It was supposed to bake for thirty minutes and because of a smudge of batter on the recipe page, Dad thought it said an hour and thirty minutes!" Emilia said.

"I'll never forget the look on Dad's face after the smoke cleared," said Alfie.

"That cake was so burned it looked like coal!" Emilia added.

"Mom had to save the day by picking up a cake at Sweet Life Bakery," Alfie remembered. "It was good, but it wasn't as good as this."

"Yeah, this is the best cake ever." Emilia scraped the rest of the chocolate frosting from her plate.

The band was going into their final song of the night. Alfie caught Nanette's and Teddy's eyes as they played and waved to them onstage. He popped the last bite of cake into his mouth. Just then, he felt his world shift a little bit. He gave one last look around the club at all the laughing, dancing, eating, and very happy people before . . .

Chapter 17

... He was suddenly back in his kitchen at home, standing next to Zia Donatella. She was just finishing up her bowl of gumbo, as if nothing had happened and no time had passed. But Alfie only needed to see Emilia's face to know that yes, something had happened—again.

"You know, I was thinking—" Zia started to say.

"Wait!" Alfie cried. "How long were we gone?" It was all so crazy. Seconds ago they were in a jazz club in New Orleans—now they were back.

Zia cocked her head to one side and said, *"Che vuoi dire?* What do you mean?"

"Ziiiaaa . . . ," Emilia said, drawing out her name.

Zia had the most innocent look on her face. "I don't know what you're talking about."

Alfie laughed and shook his head. Zia was impossible! Someday he'd figure it out. But for now, he guessed he'd just keep on enjoying the adventures.

"Anyway," Zia said, "I was thinking about our conversation during the picnic today—of all the different places we all want to visit. Maybe we need to start making a list."

"Good idea!" Alfie said. He had more ideas than he could count.

"There is so much to see and do in your own country and in mine. Italy is *mi casa*, my home," Zia continued. "But there is always something new I can discover there."

"I want to see the Colosseum in Rome," Emilia said.

"I want to go boating on Lake Como," Alfie said.

"See? *Esattamente*, exactly!" said Zia. "And I want to visit San Francisco, and your dad wants to go mountain biking in the Rockies."

"That does sound pretty awesome," Alfie said.

"So much to see and do," Zia repeated. "And so important to take time and really understand what makes each place special."

"But that's the problem," said Alfie. "There are so many places here in the US and around the world. How will we ever see—and taste—it all?"

Zia smiled with a hint of magic in her eyes. "We'll just have to take it one city at a time. Now, let me think—what should be *primeiro* on the list?"

A Note from Giada

When I think of New Orleans, I hear trumpets blaring and see people dancing through the streets with bright beads dangling from beautiful wrought iron balconies. I think of a colorful city that has almost every type of architecture imaginable, from Creole cottages to grand mansions, from the French Quarter to skyscrapers reaching up into the clouds. This city is steeped in so much history that it's impossible not to turn a corner and run into a story about its past.

The real reason I love New Orleans? It is a melting pot not only of cultures but of foods and tastes. It's what makes New Orleans one of the top food destinations in the whole world. There is a pride carried throughout the city for its mixed culture that is directly reflected in the food—and that's why you can't find this food anywhere but New Orleans, like beignets, gumbo, or étouffée. It kind of reminds me of Italy in that way, which I love.

Visit New Orleans hungry, ready to dance through the streets, and with a desire to learn about its history. Each time I go, it's like the very first time!